Text copyright © 2013 by Mac Barnett • Illustrations copyright © 2013 by Kevin Cornell

First Edition • 10 9 8 7 6 5 4 3 2 • G615-7693-2-13269 • Printed in China
Library of Congress Cataloging-in-Publication Data
Barnett, Mac.
  Count the monkeys / by Mac Barnett and Kevin Cornell.—1st ed.
       p. cm.
  Summary: The reader is invited to count the animals that have frightened the monkeys off the pages.
  ISBN 978-1-4231-6065-6
  [1. Animals—Fiction. 2. Monkeys—Fiction. 3. Counting. 4. Humorous stories.] I. Cornell, Kevin, ill. II. Title.
  PZ7.B26615Cp 2013
  [Fic]—dc23   2012020299

Book design by Whitney Manger • Reinforced binding • Visit www.disneyhyperionbooks.com

For Kate Sherwood
—M.B.

For Kim, who holds my hand.
—K.C.

MONKEYS
THIS WAY→

Hey, kids! Time to count the monkeys!

It's fun. It's easy. All you have to do is turn the page . . .

and

COUNT
THE
MONKEYS

MAC
BARNETT

KEVIN
CORNELL

Disney • Hyperion Books
New York

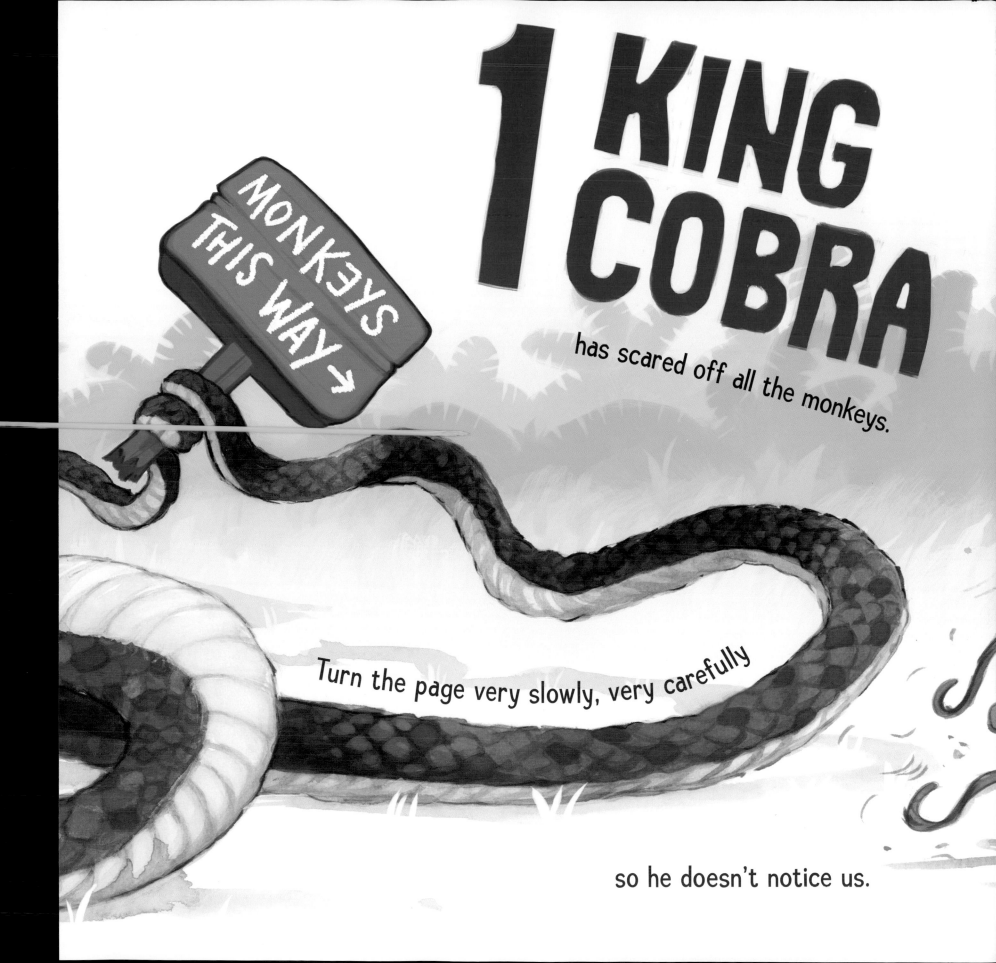

1 KING COBRA

MONKƎYS THIS WAY →

has scared off all the monkeys.

Turn the page very slowly, very carefully

so he doesn't notice us.

Or is that **2 MONGEESE?**

I am pretty sure it is

2 MONGOOSES.

Let's vote.

Raise your hand if you think it's mongooses.
Now raise your hand if you think it's mongeese.

Interesting.

Turn the page—I bet the monkeys will come back.

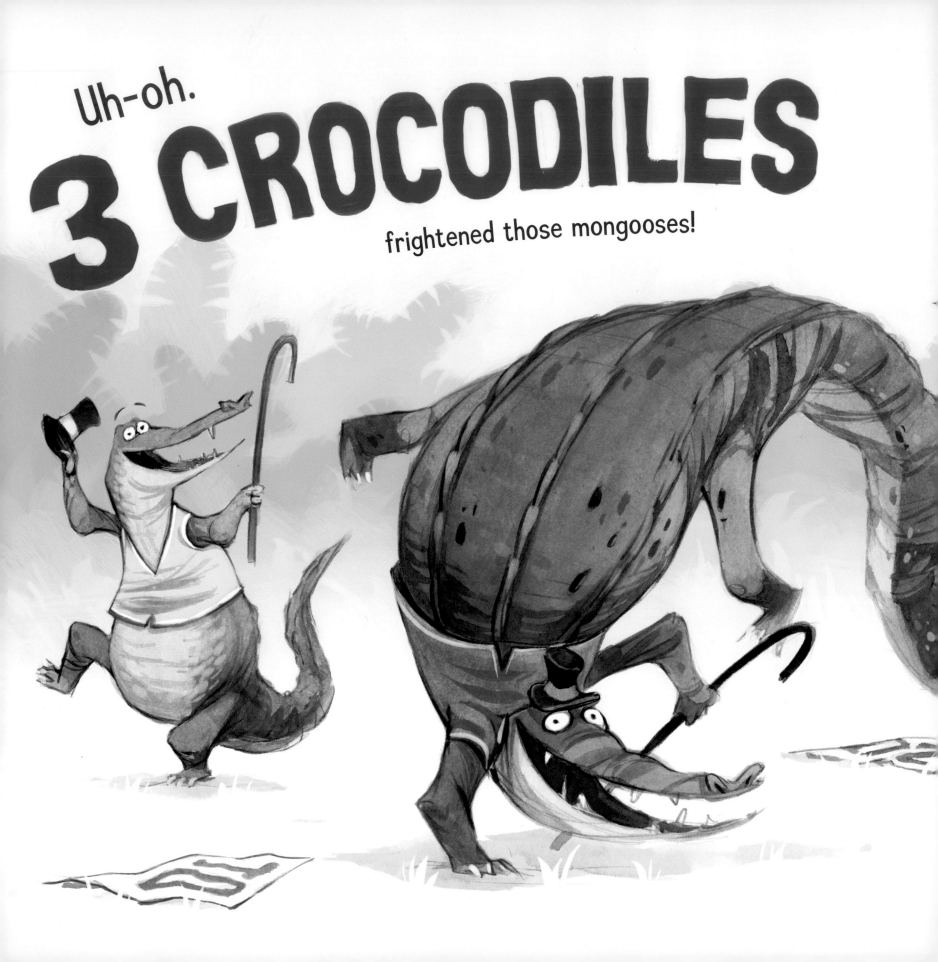

Uh-oh.
3 CROCODILES

frightened those mongooses!

I dislike crocodiles, especially **these crocodiles.**

Move your hand in a *zigzag*

while you
turn the page—

it will confuse them.

I never thought I would miss those crocodiles, but these **4 GRIZZLY BEARS** are even worse!

We're never going to count the monkeys!

Okay. Put your arms above your head! Make a loud roar! Bang together some pots and pans, if you have them.

BUT MOST IMPORTANTLY, TURN THAT PAGE!

OH NO!
5 BEE SWARMS
drove off those bears.

Bees can smell fear.

Phew!

6 SWEET OLD BEEKEEPERS

have shooed off all those bees.

Say "thank you" six times, very politely—
these ladies care about good manners.

Now, finally, the monkeys can come back.

Turn the page and count the monkeys!

Wolves and grandmas never get along!

This is very important: **Don't look** these wolves in the eyes.

In fact, cover your eyes while you turn the page.

Thanks, guys!
Now it's safe for the monkeys.

Give each lumberjack
a high five
and then turn the page

so we can

COUNT
THE
MONKEYS.

Tell these guys
"SCRAM!"

Say it even
LOUDER!

Good. Let's turn the page.

Look at that!

10 POLKA-DOTTED RHINOCEROSES WITH BAGPIPES AND BAD BREATH cleared out those lumberjacks.

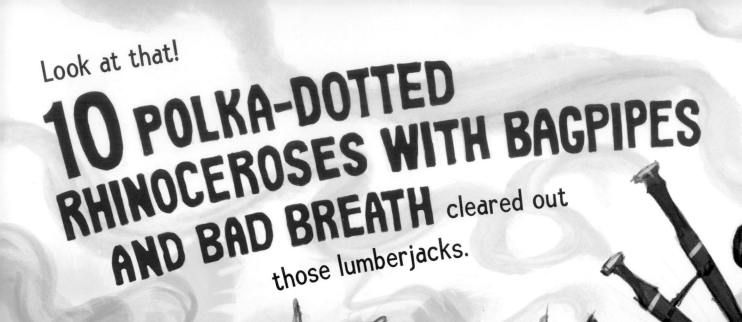

Okay! We're finally ready to—
Oh no. It looks like we're
out of pages.

This is terrible!
We made it to the end
and there are

O MONKEYS

in this book.

Now we'll never get to count the monkeys.